Katharine's Doll

by Elizabeth Winthrop

illustrated by Marylin Hafner

A Unicorn Book • E. P. Dutton • New York

Some Other Books by Elizabeth Winthrop

I Think He Likes Me
Sloppy Kisses
Marathon Miranda
Miranda in the Middle
Journey to the Bright Kingdom

Text copyright © 1983 by Elizabeth Winthrop Mahony
Illustrations copyright © 1983 by Marylin Hafner

Library of Congress Cataloging in Publication Data

Winthrop, Elizabeth.
  Katharine's doll.

  (A Unicorn book)
  Summary: After quarreling over a doll, two girls
come to realize that people make the best friends.
  [1. Friendship—Fiction.   2. Dolls—Fiction]
I. Hafner, Marylin, ill.   II. Title.   III. Series.
PZ7.W768Kat   1983   [E]   83-1408
ISBN 0-525-44061-5

Published in the United States by E. P. Dutton, Inc.,
2 Park Avenue, New York, N.Y. 10016

Published simultaneously in Canada by Clarke,
Irwin & Company Limited, Toronto and Vancouver

Editor: Emilie McLeod   Designer: Isabel Warren-Lynch

Printed in the U.S.A.   First Edition
10 9 8 7 6 5 4 3 2 1

for Carey and Eliza, two good friends
E. W.

to Emilie McLeod, in loving memory
M. H.

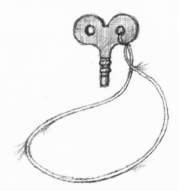

Molly was Katharine's best friend.
Katharine was Molly's best friend.
They walked to school together in the morning. They went roller-skating together in the afternoon. They kept each other's secrets. They brushed each other's hair.

Katharine taught Molly how to sing
"Miss Mary Mack" when they jumped rope.

Molly taught Katharine how to play
"Chopsticks" on the piano.
They even wore the same size shoes.

One day, Katharine got a new doll from
her grandmother. It was the most beautiful
doll Katharine had ever seen. It had soft
brown hair that felt like real hair. It had
big blue eyes that opened very slowly.
It had a soft body that felt just like a
real baby's.

Katharine called Molly. "Come down to my
house," she said. "My grandmother sent me
a new doll. She is beautiful. I have named
her Charlotte."

So Molly came running to Katharine's house.
"Can I hold her?" Molly asked.
"Just a minute," Katharine said. "I want
to change her dress."

"See the way her eyes open and close?
She looks like a real baby, doesn't she?"
  Molly nodded.
  Katharine took off the doll's sundress
and put on a party dress.

Then she took all her old dolls out of
the baby carriage and put them on the floor.
"There, Charlotte," she said. "You fit just
right."

"You didn't let me hold her," Molly said.
"Oops, I forgot," Katharine said. "I'll
let you hold her later."

Molly and Katharine took
Charlotte for a walk around
the block.

Katharine let Molly push
the carriage half the time.

When they got back to the house,
Katharine let Molly hold Charlotte.
"Hold her head up," said Katharine.
"She feels just like a real baby," Molly
whispered.
"I told you so," Katharine said.

Katharine took Charlotte away from Molly.
"It's time for her dinner."
    "It's time for me to go home," said Molly.
    Katharine was so busy she forgot to say good-bye.

Every day, Molly and Katharine played
with Charlotte. They changed her diapers
and fed her lunch and dressed her up and
took her for walks.

Sometimes Katharine
let Molly fix Charlotte's
food.

Sometimes Katharine
let Molly change
Charlotte's diapers.

Sometimes Katharine even let Molly rock
Charlotte to sleep.

But Molly always wanted to hold Charlotte
more. "I wish you were mine," she whispered
to Charlotte very softly, so Katharine did not
hear her.

When Katharine decided
to give Charlotte a bath,
she told Molly to turn on
the water. "But don't make
it too hot."

Molly filled the sink with
water.

"Bring me the towel, and we'll
wrap her up," said Katharine.

Molly got the towel and
held out her arms.

"You can carry her to the sink,"
Katharine said, "but I want to
give her the bath."

"You can give her the bath if you
let me dress her," Molly said.
"Wait a minute," said Katharine.
"Charlotte is my doll, you know."
They glared at each other.

"All right," Katharine said. "You can
change her dress. Then we'll put her in
the carriage, and we can go roller-skating."
"But I don't want to go roller-skating,"
said Molly. "I want to play with Charlotte."
"Who did you come here to play with?"
Katharine asked. "Me or Charlotte?"
"Charlotte," said Molly.

"You're not my friend anymore, Molly
McCook."

"You're not my friend either," Molly said.
"I'm going home."

"Go right ahead," Katharine said.

So Molly went home.

The next day, Katharine and Molly walked to school on opposite sides of the street.

After school, Katharine went to her room. She and Charlotte looked at a book together, but Katharine had to turn all the pages.

She sat Charlotte on the piano bench and they played "Chopsticks," but half the song was missing.

Katharine practiced cartwheels
in the hall.
"How about that?" she asked.

Nobody answered. Charlotte
had fallen over. She was looking
at the ceiling.

"I'm bored," Katharine said.

"Where is Molly?" asked her mother. "Isn't she coming over today?"

"We had a fight," said Katharine. "I'm never speaking to her, ever again."

"That's too bad," said her mother. "Good friends are hard to find."

"I don't need friends," said Katharine. "I've got Charlotte."

They both looked at Charlotte.
Charlotte was still looking at the ceiling.

"Why don't you go roller-skating?" said
Katharine's mother.
"All right," said Katharine, "but if I see
Molly, I'm going to stick my tongue out
at her."

So Katharine went roller-skating. She
skated up to one corner of the block.

Then she skated down to the other corner.

    She skated past Molly's house and stuck
out her tongue at the front door.
    The front door opened. Molly walked down
the steps. She sat down and put on her
roller skates.

Katharine watched her. "If you're going to skate here," Katharine said, "I guess I'll have to skate somewhere else."

"That's just fine with me," Molly said. "I don't like to skate with people who stick out their tongues."

"Well I don't like to skate with people who like their best friend's doll better than their best friend."

"I never said that," Molly said.

"You did too," Katharine said.

Molly stood up and started to skate down the block.

Katharine zoomed past her.
Molly fell down and burst out crying.
"You're mean, Katharine Murphy," she yelled.

"I didn't do it on purpose,"
Katharine said.
"I bet you did," Molly said.
"No I didn't," Katharine said.
She helped Molly up.

"You want to come to my house
and play?" Katharine said.
Molly sniffed. "I don't know,"
she said.
"Please, Molly," Katharine said.
"I'm bored playing all by myself."
"Me too," said Molly. "At least
you've got Charlotte."

"Charlotte can't play the piano," said
Katharine.

"That's right," said Molly. "And Charlotte
can't jump rope."

"Or do cartwheels," said Katharine.

"Or sing 'Miss Mary Mack,'" said Molly.

"Or keep a secret," said Katharine.

"Or be a best friend," said Molly.

j
Fic   Mayer, Marianna
May   The Brambleberrys
      animal book of colors

Fic
May

For Kendall

Copyright © 1987 by Marianna Mayer and Gerald McDermott
All rights reserved
Published by Bell Books
Boyds Mills Press, Inc.
A Highlights Company
910 Church Street
Honesdale, Pennsylvania 18431
Originally published by Riverbank Press

Publisher Cataloging-in-Publication Data

Mayer, Marianna.
   The Brambleberrys animal book of colors/by Marianna Mayer; illustrated by
Gerald McDermott.
   28p. : col. ill. ; cm.
Summary: A picture book introduction to colors.
ISBN 1-878093-76-2
1. Colors—Juvenile Literature. [1. Colors.] I. McDermott, Gerald, ill. II. Title.
[E]   1991
LC Card Number 91-70418

THE BRAMBLEBERRYS is a Trademark of Riverbank Press

Distributed by St. Martin's Press
Printed in Hong Kong
Produced by Blaze IPI

THE BRAMBLEBERRYS ANIMAL BOOK OF
COLORS

Created by
Marianna Mayer
and
Gerald McDermott

A RIVERBANK PRESS BOOK

BELL BOOKS

WHITE

RED

BLACK

GREEN

YELLOW

ORANGE

BROWN

GRAY

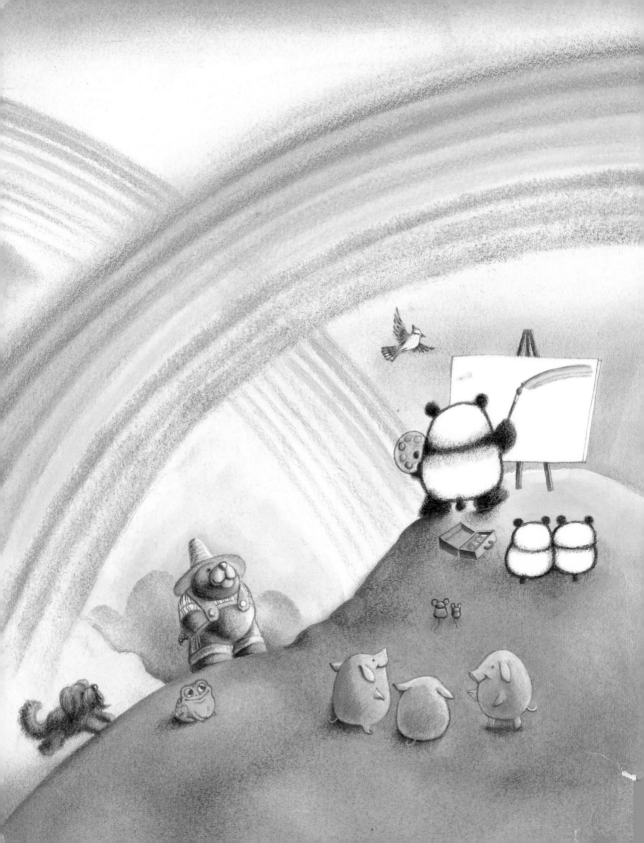